I Know A Goldfish That Can't Swim

By Andy Baines

Published by New Generation Publishing in 2012

Copyright © Andy Baines 2012

First Edition

The author asserts the moral right under the Copyright, Designs and Patents Act 1988 to be identified as the author of this work.

All Rights reserved. No part of this publication may be reproduced, stored in a retrieval system or transmitted, in any form or by any means without the prior consent of the author, nor be otherwise circulated in any form of binding or cover other than that which it is published and without a similar condition being imposed on the subsequent purchaser.

www.newgeneration-publishing.com

New Generation **Publishing**

To Lisa, Joel and Oliver.

Thank you for believing, thank you for laughing and thank you for your inspiration.

My Appreciation to:

Sally Lee. *A friend and colleague who has helped massively in the checking and constant correction of my work – Thank You*

To the five pupils and one staff member of Tibshelf Community School for the extraordinary artwork used in the book
- Thank You

Corrina Holyoake. *For an eye-catching masterpiece that is the front cover.*
- Thank You

Front Cover by Corrina Holyoake

www.corrinascreations.co.uk

Additional Artwork Produced by pupils of Tibshelf Community School:

Holly Tudor
'Clever Dog Part 1'
'Clever Dog Part 2'
'Lucky Underpants'

Holly Peternel
'Bored'
'How Did The Hippo Get To Rio?"
'PE'

Lucas King
'Spell For The Wicked'
'The Head Teacher'
' An Alternative Twelve Days Of Christmas'

Samson Tudor
'Cycling Fish Part 1'
'Cycling Fish Part 2'
'Short And Shorter Stories'

Lenina Scott
'Help Your Brother'
'Bath Time'
'The Effects Of Red Sauce'

And **Hilary Smith**, friend and colleague,
'Boris'
'Sharks In The Pond'
'Cyril The Squirrel '

Foreword

From a young age I have always fancied myself as a writer; not a good one, but still a writer. Over the years I have written silly poems and stories to support lessons and to entertain my own children. Some children have giggled, some laughed and others have stared in disbelief - disbelief at how bad a poem has been. So, I thought I would put some together and share some with you. Especially the very bad ones.

All these poems are written about children, for children. Some are based on the children that I have been blessed with teaching. A lot of the poems are inspired by the things that I have heard from my own children. A few of the poems are based on incidents that happened to me when I was a wee lad at school too.

Thank you for choosing to buy this book (a very wise choice). The proceeds of this book will be used to develop my Goldfish School of Excellence, for Goldfish with Talent. The school is due to open in 2013 and is set to rival Oxford and Cambridge universities, so watch out for a boat full of fish in the 2014 boat race. (There's a poem in the making somewhere).

Cycling Fish (Part 1)

I know a goldfish that can't swim
It sits there at the bottom of the tank.
He forgot to wear a rubber ring;
That is why he sank.

I know a goldfish that can't swim
He has lessons at the local pool.
To see a fish in armbands:
It really is quite cool.

I know a goldfish that can't swim
He's given swimming its final chance.
He has now taken up cycling,
And is training for the Tour de France.

He is not a fantastic cyclist.
Not by any quarter.
To see him ride on his bike:
He's like a fish out of water.

Prune Powered Spoon

It was just around noon,
In the middle of June, when
I decided to fly to the moon.

To the moon?
In June?
Just around noon?

Noon, June, moon … on a spoon.

On a spoon?
To the moon?
In June?
Just around noon?

Yes.
Off to the moon.
On a prune powered spoon.
Fired by harpoon,
Whilst playing pontoon,
With a baboon and racoon from Rangoon
Who was playing bassoon.

Off to the moon?
On a prune powered spoon?
Fired by harpoon?
Whilst playing pontoon?
With a baboon and racoon from Rangoon?
Who was playing bassoon?

Yes.
Noon, June, moon. Prune powered spoon. Harpoon, pontoon, baboon. Racoon from Rangoon, playing bassoon.

See you soon.

Love a buffoon.

(Now read quicker)

Clever Dog (Part 1)

My dog is very clever,
He doesn't bark – he talks.
I do not put him on a lead,
He takes himself for walks.

Collects the post and paper.
He even does the crossword.
It's almost unbelievable:
Absolutely, just absurd!

He doesn't eat dog food,
He likes to cook his own.
He does not chase sticks,
Or like to bury bones.

He answers the phone,
Whenever it rings.
He knows all sorts of facts,
About a hundred different things!

He likes to watch the television,
Especially if it's a quiz.
He is fantastically clever,
My dog's a real whizz.

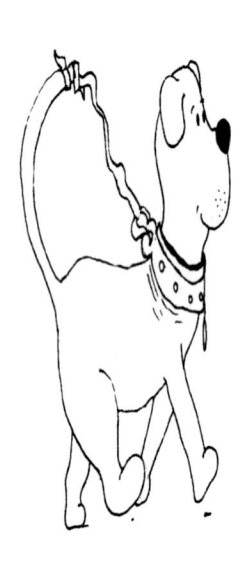

Sharks In The Pond

Well, there are no ducks on the pond,
It's a really eerie park.
There must be something in the water,
Like a vicious, nasty shark.

No ducks will go near,
Not even for Hovis bread.
There must be something in the pond,
The poor ducks really dread.

I don't want to scare the other kids,
It just isn't my style,
In fact, it's probably not a shark …
Just a CROCODILE!!

The Peculiar Case Of Wilber G. Chase

The peculiar case of Wilber G. Chase
Is sure to get people talking around the place.

In 1907 he took part in a Pole expedition -
But he was a mad man, by his very own admission.

He took off on his sledge
Giving a most boastful, promise and pledge:

'On my return, my ladies and lords,
I will bring you the most valuable hoards.'

'I do not refer to jewels or gold
But a creature from times and stories of old.'

'I shall be the first to capture the beast
That roams freely through North, South, West and East'

'Full of cunning is my plan…
… I will find the abominable snowman'

As Chase left into the dimming light
Unfortunately, history he did not write.

Many years passed without a so - much - as - a - trace
No one knows what happened to Wilber G. Chase

Many went in search of Chase;
They had almost given up hope on the case.

Some 20 years or longer had passed
When news arrived with a blast from the past.

An Eskimo chap, Inuit of sorts
Came skiing and offering unsubstantiated reports:

'This old Chase fellow man you seek
Weird, wonderful, barmy – unique.'

'Lives some hundred miles North-West from here -
He is somewhat of a failing pioneer.'

'He wishes not to return without fame
And hope you may pardon his name.'

'This is to be his wish,
As the abominable snowman doesn't exist.'

So to you he has kept his grace,
And leave to you his travelling case.'

Where had the case and Chase been? No one knew.
In the end what could anyone do?

In the Arctic he may still wander
While folk here occasionally, but not often ponder:

On the peculiar case of one Wilber G Chase.

Bath Time

My bum got burned in the bath.
It seemed all right on my toes.
My bum was like a barbecued burger
And steam blew out my nose!

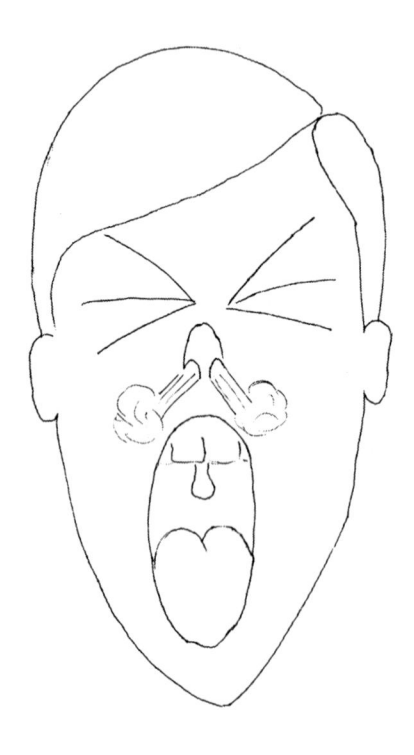

Healthy Eating

Fruit and veg:
Eat five a day,
But be sure to stand
A safe distance away.

Although much healthier
You are bound to be.
Stand to the front,
And not behind me.

Apples, bananas,
Broccoli and cauliflower:
All very potent
But, give you great power.

You will start to feel better,
Right from the start.
Spontaneously armed,
With the deadliest fart!

Help Your Brother

Don't put your brother in the
Washing machine.
It's not the best way to get him clean!

Don't put your brother to dry in the
Microwave.
It's not the best way – please behave!

And don't put your brother on the
Washing line.
Or use the furniture polish to make him shine!

Just put him in the bath.
Get him some soap.
And just stop acting like a dope!

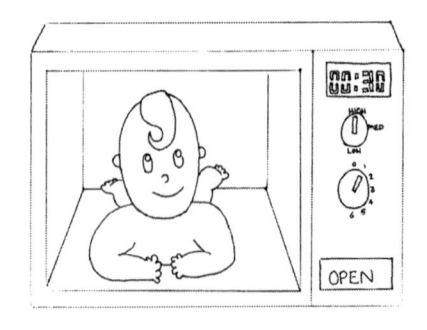

Twozzletonk

Twozzletonk and other such words,
Can be used in grace with Wosterylink.
You can include them anywhere,
No matter what Fanaloolas think!

Describing folk as Jiggerytolka,
An incruptious word to use.
But the very best by a country mile:
Is - Nickerknockerrockerchews!

Having Pets

"Will you feed the hamster?"
So I did - to the cat!

"Will you feed the fish?"
So I did – to the cat!

"Will you feed the cat?"
So I did – to the dog!

"Will you feed the dog?"
Lucky for the dog, he's not hungry!

Twelve Sugars Sid

Twelve Sugars Sid
Has twelve sugars in his tea.
He even has sugar,
On toast and spaghetti!

Twelve Sugars Sid
Has twelve sugars on his bread.
He just loves sugar,
He will have it on cheese spread.

Twelve Sugars Sid
Has twelve sugars on roast beef.
He scoops it on potatoes,
We just stare in disbelief!

Twelve Sugars Sid
Has twelve sugars on all pasta.
Will his brand new teeth last?
Or will they fall out faster?

Mmmm Ear Wax!

If you're feeling peckish,
And your tummy starts to rumble,
Put a finger in your ear,
And let it have a fumble.

On the end of your digit,
Is a yellow tasty speck.
Don't hesitate and wolf it down,
Slide it down your neck.

Or, chew it nice and slowly,
Tongue it 'round your mouth with 'welly.'
Then take a great big swallow,
And down into your belly.

It tastes a little peculiar,
And in your throat may stick.
But if you're really lucky –
You'll taste it again when sick!

Cycling Fish (Part 2)

I know a goldfish that can't swim
He took up cycling, but it wasn't his sport.
It was difficult turning the pedals,
Because his fins were too weak and too short.

I know a goldfish that can't swim
He can be found on his local golf course.
He can clobber the ball for miles,
His fins generating maximum force.

I know a goldfish that can't swim
With golf he gave his full concentration.
He drives the ball straight to the hole,
He's an accurate, golfing sensation.

I know a goldfish that can't swim
He played Tiger Woods just for fun.
Winning titles left, right and centre,
Every tournament he entered he won!

An Angry Bee

At the bottom of our garden,
There lies a massive tree.
It's home to lots of insects,
And an angry bumble bee.

If you go too near,
Be sure to run, old chum;
The angry bee has just one thought:
To sting you on the bum!

Bored

I'm so bored I could…could… turn into… superman.
I would then grab my teacher by a trouser leg and and arm.

I'd shout (to cheers from my classmates) 'enough is enough' or ' the boredom you have created with your evil boredom power is mind numbing!'
Swinging him through 1080 degrees before,
Letting him fly through the window, beyond the known universe into to a galaxy far, far away.

But I cant: I'm not Clark Kent, therefore I'm not superman

And I would end up in detention and mum would not be pleased with that!

Otherwise – a fool proof plan!

My Top Ten Top Favourite Foods are:

1. Chocolate
2. Mars Bar
3. Mini Mars Miniature Heroes
4. Snack sized Mars
5. Mars Ice Cream Bars
6. Mars Chocolate Milk shake
7. Kit Kat 2 fingered
8. Kit Kat 4 fingered
9. Kit Kat Chunky
10. Crunchy
11. Ice Cream (chocolate, with chocolate chips)

Tom's Mum

We were playing on the playground. It was playtime and that's what we do – play.
A fighter jet plane flew over our playground.
The noise was thunderous.
The infants ran for cover. A new starter nearly cried!
The teacher spilled her coffee and dropped her biscuits.
One was a custard cream. Not sure what the other one was, but if I had to guess, I'd go for a digestive of some sort.
Tom said that it was his mum.
I didn't believe him and said, ' Tom I don't believe you.'
But he was sure it was his mum and said, ' I'm sure that's my mum'.
He said that she was going shopping.
It was a Tuesday and she always shops on a Tuesday.
'Fair enough' I said.
And we carried on playing.

PE

I have a love hate relationship with PE.
I love the lessons.
But I hate getting changed and here is why:

1. Everyone laughing at my matching Action Man pants and vest.
2. I always put either my jumper or shirt on inside out.
3. I put my trousers on back to front.
4. When I put my trousers on the right way they usually belong to someone else: too tight, too short.
5. I'm the only boy to have Velcro shoes.

So think of me every Wednesday and Friday when I have to teach the wretched lesson.

...WRONG WAY ROUND!

YAY!...

...SOMEBODY ELSE'S!

Hello

'Hello, hello, hello
And how do you do?
I'm sorry I do not know your name.
Pardoning me, who are you?'

'Hello, hello, hello to you
And how do you do?
I am Lady Primrose Jupiter-Smythe.
Pardoning me, who are you?'

'Very sorry my dear Lady,
I'm Baron James Von Snitzel-Smee,
I am very pleased to meet you Lady Smythe.
Would you care to Tango with me?'

The Baron and the Lady,
Danced all night whilst stars shone bright.
But soon came the time for parting,
Alas, it came to the end of the night.

'Goodnight, goodnight, goodnight
My sweet lady oh so fair.
I hope we get to meet again,
Until then please take care.'

'Goodnight, goodnight, goodnight to you
So fine a gent, I met by chance.
I too hope we meet again,
And have the opportunity to dance.'

Swimming Day

Standing by the pool,
It is time to take the dip.
This is one activity,
I'd really like to skip.

It always makes me feel off,
After – I'm just not right.
I'm forever sneezing,
And a sorry, poorly sight.

The water is freezing cold,
It goes in my nose and ears.
My goggles start to steam up,
And I can't see very clear.

I feel like I am sinking,
I'm tired of being wet.
I have swallowed half the water,
And not even at the end yet.

We have to take cold showers,
Wait for the coach and freeze.
I stand and start to shiver,
In the blustery winter breeze.
I know at school I'll struggle,
I won't be able to follow.
I think I have the flu,
It is getting hard to swallow.

I will have to take some time off,
To get over this disease.
Just because of swimming,
For a week I'll continuously sneeze.

If I Ruled Schools

Do my homework, behave in schools -
If I was in charge, I would change the rules:

School starts at anytime.
Being late is not a crime.

Homework is banished, no mistake.
And I would add an extra break.

Go to school on every other day.
Forget the teachers, it's us you pay.

A longer weekend, three days or more.
(While ever at home not even one chore).

Teachers are not allowed to shout,
And no longer throw orders about.

McDonalds provide the school dinner,
If for free, a sure fire winner.

The school holiday system is a mess.
We would have much longer, due to stress.

So, children all across the land,
Join me as I make my stand.

Put me in charge of all your schools,
I will promise you, you'll have these rules!

Boris

I have a pet spider called Boris,
He lives in our garden shed.
He has eight long hairy legs,
And a gigantic, enormous head.

His favourite food is fish and chips,
He is also fond of mustard.
For dessert he likes apple pie,
Covered in cold custard.

A Poem For Girls

Boys like football,
Girls like pop,
Boys are bottom
Girls are top.

Boys aren't sensible,
Girls see sense,
Boys play 'tiggy',
Girls chat against the fence.

Boys do little,
Girls work a lot,
Boys save money,
Girls lose the plot.

Boys like spikes,
Girls like curls,
Boys are boys,
And girls are girls!

Cyril The Squirrel

Cyril the squirrel from Wirral,
Was climbing to the top of his tree.
He fell, hitting every branch,
Seriously damaging his knee.

Cyril the squirrel from Wirral,
Due to the swelling and the cuts.
Really had difficulty,
When trying to bury his nuts.

My Pet Monster

There is a monster in my bedroom,
He's a real 'scaredy cat',
He doesn't like the dark,
He's frightened of this, and that.

He's frightened of his shadow,
He jumps at his own reflection,
He needs lots of love and care,
Some tenderness and affection.

At night he jumps into my bed,
And snuggles out of sight;
He can only sleep safe at night,
If I cuddle him, real tight!

My School Photo

My school photo came back today,
I really look absurd;
My hair is all glued to the side,
I look just like a nerd.

My eyes are half shut,
It wasn't worth the while,
My face looks fake and plastic,
With a 'Wallace and Gromit' smile.

I tried to look happy,
I tried to do a pose,
Oh No! I've just noticed,
There's something up my nose!!

I know they will still want it,
On the cabinet, in its place,
And so for the next few years,
We'll be looking at my face!

But Do I Want To Be A Bee?

I hate Friday mornings.
We do literacy.
It really bores me silly;
I'd rather be a bee.

I'd buzz around the garden,
Smelling all the flowers.
Whizzing 'round in madness,
Having fun for hours.

I might collect some pollen.
Or do a naughty thing.
Find a lonely little boy:
His bottom I might sting.

Then, reality claws me back.
Me, a bee – quite funny:
I really do not like flying,
And I hate the smell of honey.

I Hate Monday Mornings

I hate Monday mornings,
They make me feel so bad,
I really do get quite depressed;
In fact, incredibly sad.

Five more days to count down,
The week has just begun;
I can't wait until Friday night,
Then I'll have some fun.

(By The Teacher)

A Teacher's Poem

Why are my children gormless?
They sit in class like frogs;
I would get a better response,
From a classroom full of logs.

I'd be better talking to the wall,
A classroom full of bricks.
The cleverest thing in their heads,
Are the nits and fleas and tics.

I'm sorry if I offend you,
But this is how I see;
Spend just a minute with my class:
You'll sympathise with me.

A Spell For The Wicked
(Works best on a full moon)

Wing of bat,
Eye of newt,
Mouldy socks,
Rotten old fruit.

Toe nail clippings,
Mouse's tail,
Engine oil,
Shell of snail.

Mix together
With salt and blood,
Boil for one hour,
Add a spoonful of mud.

Drink it quick,
On midnight hour,
Through your veins,
Feel the power.

It tastes vile,
Ignore the bad smell,
If you want to be wicked,
Follow this spell.

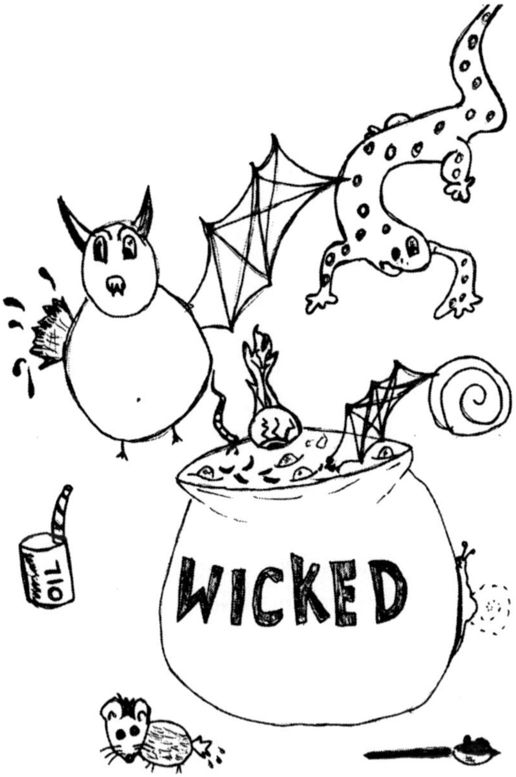
WICKED
OIL

A Poem For Spoilt Kids

Do you wear designer clothes?
Bet your mother even wipes your nose.
And in the morning your bed is made,
As you walk downstairs, your breakfast laid.
Can you go to school without help?
Or do you cry at the gate and yelp?
Do you sit and stare into space
With a blank expression on your face?
Maybe throw a 'paddy' until the teacher will come,
Hoping he'll do all for you, just like your mum.
But he says "get on with it dear,
Or you will be spending your break time in here."
And you'll go home and have a moan,
Whimper, mardy, have a groan.
You just think life is unfair,
Stand up for yourself – we don't care!
So, get on with it and stand up tall;
If not, you'll have no friends at all.

The New Boy Is A Wild Child

The new boy, Tom, is really strange,
If I was him I'd try and change,
You'd try to impress, keep your head down,
Not act the fool or be the clown.
After a couple of minutes, he burst his bubble:
He said rude words and got in to trouble.
At break he made the Head Teacher wrench,
When he hopped and skipped across the bench.
He called Christian for being ginger and small,
Mrs. Baxter put him on the wall.
And then he said it wasn't him,
Luckily, Mrs Baxter isn't dim.
He was told to head off upstairs,
But I don't think he really cares.
When he got back he wasn't worried,
Back to the wall, he stubbornly scurried;
Only to turn and pull a face.
This new kid's an absolute disgrace.
At toilet break he turned to me,
''Next person in, I'll cover in wee.''
I don't think this kid will last the year,
If he's not careful he will be out of here.

Hamster On The Run

The school hamster escaped,
It must have run away.
I don't think it wanted to hang around,
Because of spelling test that day.

How Did The Hippo Get To Rio?
(I'll tell you how)

Travelling the world and the Seven Seas.
On a hippopotamus and a family of fleas.
Crossing the planet far and wide,
Up mountain, 'cross plains, upon a high tide.

Through desert dunes for many a mile,
Sight-seeing tours on the river Nile.
A hippo and fleas climbing Himalayas tall,
Trekking to China and walking the Wall.

Hippo, fleas and me, crossing frontiers,
Now weighed down with collected souvenirs.
To Northern outposts, empty, good for the soul;
A chance meeting with Santa by the North Pole.

The Hippo and me, we were coping well.
The fleas were tired, it was starting to tell.
Each day they struggled under new skies.
They were slowly passing, dropping like flies.

So the Hippo and me took them to a retreat.
A place to relax and put up their feet.
We decided to stay, fleas, me and hippo:
You can find us beached in the sun of Rio.

The Effects Of Red Sauce

Daniel eats red sauce on bread,
He says it helps his brain and head.
It is all he eats, even on his cornflakes,
His favourite drink is red sauce milkshake!
I wonder if this could be so:
The reason Daniel doesn't grow.
I think that this tomato sauce,
Has some weird, unusual force.
Daniel's nine years old and two foot three,
And has tomato smelling, orange coloured wee!

It's Been A Long Time

A day is a long time:
24 hours.
"It's been a long day."
24 hours, same as yesterday!

A week is an even longer time:
7 days.
"It's been a long week."
7 days, same as last week!

A year is an even longer time:
52 weeks; 12 months; 365.25days.
"It's been a long year."
52 week; 12 months; 365.25 days, same as last year!

Stink Bomb

At the school disco, during the slow dance,
Oliver saw his opportunity and took a great big chance:
He rolled a stink bomb across the room,
It exploded under a bench.
The only thing staying in the room,
Was the dreadful stench!

The smell almost lifted the ceiling,
Girls complained of a peculiar feeling.
Quickly the crowd began to part,
All because of Oliver's fake fart!

The Dodo And Extinction

Why the Dodo died out no one knows;
This is my theory and here it goes:

The Dodo came from the island of Mauritius.
It got jealous and rather over ambitious.
The Dodo so wanted to soar up above
Like a swallow, an eagle, pigeon or dove.

The Dodo would climb the tallest cliff or tree
This time it would fly – well - not quite
maybe.

Failure followed failure until the last – well
you know
Extinct, dead as… erm …a Dodo!

Clever Dog (Part 2)

My dog went on a quiz.
It was called 'The Weakest Link.'
He answered every question,
He didn't have to think.

Anne Robinson tried to trick him.
She claimed he was barking mad.
Yet he banked the most money,
So he wasn't doing bad.

My dog won round after round.
It sent Anne to despair.
As he answered more questions,
She began to pull out her hair.

No one voted him off.
He continued to be resilient.
Question right, after question right,
He simply was quite brilliant.

The other contestants were in shock.
It's peculiar to think:
My dog a quiz champ,
And my dog was the strongest link!

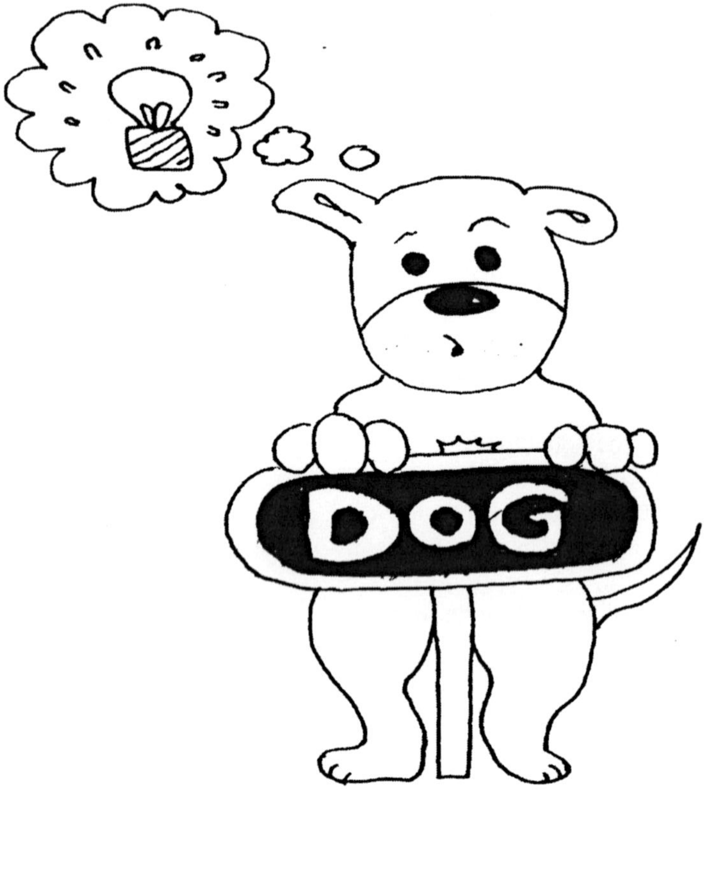
DOG

Gruesome Twosome

Billy Whizz
Drinks pop with fizz.
After one gigantic slurp,
You'll hear him burp.

His friend, Matthew McPart
Will drink fizz and fart.
These pair are just gruesome –
A bad mannered twosome.

Spamtastic Cat Stats

Eight out of twelve cats like salted ham,
Whilst at least two prefer homemade jam.
Accounting for another 2:
Rumoured like a nice beef stew.
Yet, one out of twelve cats settle for Spam.

Spellin Test

I'm getting quit gud,
I lik spelin tests,
I downt get non rong
I doo mi veri bess.

I get ten from ten,
I always get them rite,
I practis relly hard,
I lern them evry nite.

Lucky Underpants

Without my lucky underpants,
Things go horribly wrong.
I have to wear them everyday.
One day my mum washed them:
I got all my spellings wrong.

On a football match day they went missing:
We lost 9-0, I scored an own goal, missed a penalty and
one of my shots knocked out my grandma who was
stood near the corner flag. She now has one of her front
teeth missing.

Whilst on holiday, my dad made me take them off to go
swimming.
I jumped off the diving board… and broke my arm… in
two places.

However, when I have them on, the world is a different
place.
I put my hand down the sofa, searching for the TV
remote.
I found a £20 note.

I went to McDonalds.
I once again had on my lucky pants.
I got a Big Mac, large fries, shake and a McFlurry – all
free.

I went to the cinema.
Guess who sat next to me?
David Beckham.
Things got even better.
Two minutes later.
Guess who sat the other side of me?

Simon Cowell.
And he even shared his popcorn.

I have tried to explain this lucky pants situation to my parents,
But they insist I can't wear them everyday.
So next weekend I'm wearing my lucky underpants,
And going to buy 365 pairs of lucky pants.

Staff Room Ghost

There is a ghost in the staff room,
It makes a whistling sound.
Occasionally, there is a flash of light,
Shimmering from wall to ground.
You can even see its shadow,
Hovering to and fro.
How can the teachers go in there?
I would really like to know.

I asked our teacher Mr Whyld,
He said, " There is no such thing."
What about the lights and murmurs?
And the funny kind of cling?
"Oh, don't be so foolish boy,
It's nothing like a Ghost!
It's just the photocopier!
The thing teachers use the most!"

The Head Teacher

Our Head Teacher is a dragon.
Mess with her the consequences are just dire!
One unfortunate, yet foolish child, let down her push bike tyre.
We all saw him do it.
The child denied it – what a liar!
I told you she was a dragon:
She set the child on fire!

Is Sam A Man Or Mouse?

Sam and Emily Hancock,
Have a brilliant trampoline:
Their mum bounces on it,
To get the upstairs windows clean.

They have to be so careful,
Once Sam landed on his head.
He didn't know who or where he was,
And spent several weeks in bed.

The Doctor was confused;
Poor Sam they could not sort.
But it was down to Emily,
Who had planned with quite some thought!

You see, when the incident happened,
Emily was there to nurse him in the house.
Over the next days and weeks,
She convinced Sam he was a mouse.

When the Doctor took Sam's temperature,
He would squeak and snuffle his nose.
This made Sam's condition,
Near impossible to diagnose.

Emily would bring Sam milk and cheese,
She made him frightened of the cat for real.
And now the only exercise he gets,
Is in a giant hamster wheel.

Is It In The Name?

Mars Bars, Galaxy and Milky Way have
nothing to do with space.
Chocolate mousse contains no moose.
Jelly Babies are not made of babies.
No amphibians are eaten when you have
Toad In The Hole.
Do not get me started on Shepherd's pie.
A sandwich contains no witches, or sand.
No ducks were harmed in the making of
Toilet Duck.
Mr Muscle has no muscles.
Beef Wellington has no trace of boots.
Kidney Beans have nothing to do with
your vital organs.

So please, please do not tell me that
Shampoo is the exception to this rule!

Frog And Toad

Frog and toad went to the pub,
They fancied more than flies for grub.
They had a cheese and salami sandwich with chips.

Needing a change from water,
Frog had a glass of wine.
Toad had a pint of beer.

They played darts - frog beat toad.
They played pool – toad beat frog.

Frog and toad left the pub,
Croaking drunkenly on the top of their voices.
The entire pond was woken.

Eventually, they stumbled to Frog's lily pad.
They had a cup of tea.
Frog had one sugar.
Toad had no sugar.

They chattered to the early hours of the morning.
After many cups of tea, they parted.
But agreed they should visit the pub again.

An Alternative Twelve Days Of Christmas

On the first day of Christmas, my best friend gave to me…
A runny, snotty nose.

On the second day of Christmas, my best friend gave to me…
Two black eyes and a runny, snotty nose.

On the third day of Christmas, my best friend gave to me…
Three mouldy crisps, two black eyes and a runny, snotty nose.

On the fourth day of Christmas my best friend gave to me…
Four holey socks, three mouldy crisps, two black eyes and a runny, snotty nose.

On the fifth day of Christmas my best friend gave to me…
A bout of diarrhoea, four holey socks, three mouldy crisps, two black eyes and a Runny, snotty nose.

On the sixth day of Christmas, my best friend gave to me…
Six broken pens, a bout of diarrhoea, four holey socks, three mouldy crisps, two black Eyes and a runny, snotty nose.

On the seventh day of Christmas, my best friend gave to me…

Seven fluffy sweet, six broken pens, a bout of diarrhoea, four holey socks, three Mouldy crisps, two black eyes and a runny, snotty nose.

On the eight day of Christmas, my best friend gave to me…
Eight useless stones, seven fluffy sweets, six broken pens, a bout of diarrhoea,
Four holey socks, three mouldy crisps, two black eyes and a runny, snotty nose.

On the ninth day of Christmas, my best friend gave to me…
Nine sticky bogeys, eight useless stones, seven fluffy sweets, six broken pens, a bout of Diarrhoea, four holey socks, three mouldy crisps, two black eyes and a runny, snotty Nose.

On the tenth day of Christmas, my best friend gave to me…
Ten toe nail clippings, nine sticky bogeys, eight useless stones, seven fluffy sweets, six Broken pens, a bout of diarrhoea, four holey socks, three mouldy crisps, two black Eyes and a runny, snotty nose.

On the eleventh day of Christmas, my best friend gave to me…
Eleven liquorice laces, ten toe nail clippings, nine sticky bogeys, eight useless stones, Seven fluffy sweets, six broken pens, a bout of diarrhoea, four holey socks, three Mouldy crisps, two black eyes and a runny, snotty nose.

On the twelfth day of Christmas, my best friend gave to me…

Twelve head lice, eleven liquorice laces, ten toe nail clippings, nine sticky bogeys, Eight useless stones, seven fluffy sweets, six broken pens, a bout of diarrhoea, four Holey socks, three mouldy crisps, two black eyes and a runny, snotty nose.

* Although a little, and only a little dis-tasteful, take this poem to school and beg your teacher to let your class learn and perform this song. I promise, you will have a good hard laugh until your tummy explodes!

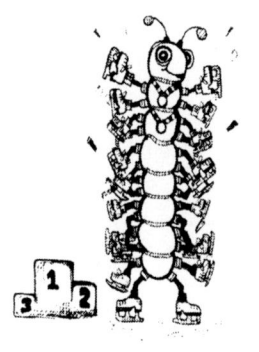

Short And Shorter Stories

A Short Story (that just so happens to be true)

Clive The Albanian Ice Skating Centipede

Clive was a huge success in his native home of Albania.

And here he was at the Winter Olympics.

His moment in the spotlight, which he didn't really enjoy. Not because of the pressure. Not because of the fans. He loved the fans. He could sign hundreds of autographs at anyone time. It was just that the spotlight dried his skin!

The dedication, the commitment, the endless hours of practise he had put in (and that was just tying the laces on his ice skating boots, not to mention untying them at the end of training).

The pain from the tumbles, the cut knees (he had kept the local chemist in business, just from plaster sales alone). The many twisted ankles, 98 to be precise, just from one innocuous fall. The constant dangers associated with the cold weather during training. I do not mean a cold or the flu, but the threat from hungry birds, desperate for a meal during the lean winter months.

So back to Clive's moment of truth – the lights in the arena dimmed. The audience silent in anticipation. The hopeful, still faces perched in front of their wide, flat, LCD, HD, 3D ready TV screens in Albania. Then came the call over the PA system:

'Representing Albania in the Mens' Figure Skating, Clive The Ice Skating Centipede.' Clive floated onto the ice accompanied by Greig's 'Morning Mood.'

First his first left foot, followed by his first right foot and then his second left foot, followed by his second right foot, and then his third left foot, followed by his third right foot, and then his fourth left foot, followed by his fourth right foot and so on and so on and so on ...

...the crowd applauded his repeated technical brilliance as he spun into the air, executing text book landing after text book landing. His gracefulness had the crowds around the world gasping. Here they were witnessing an arthropod performing a triple salko, triple lutz combination. Time stood still. All life poised - breathless. Clive was reaching for his goal. Ever since he was part of his mother's eggmass this was all he had ever dreamed of – the Olympic title.

As the gentle music continued to please the audiences' ears, Clive continued to please their eyes. With each jump, with each spin their eyes followed the centipede around the ice. At times the crowd were on their feet. Clive was like a conductor and the audience was the orchestra. His somersaults, twists and split second timing prompted them to sigh, then to gasp. Another jump with half twist into a gliding splits forced the onlookers to clap frantically and cheer. Clive was not just skating, but he was capturing the hearts of all who saw him create his masterpiece. Some people create wonderful pictures with brushes. Others create best selling books or music that spans all barriers. Clive was creating history with a show of near perfect brilliance.

The Albanian skating sensation stopped abrubtly, perfectly timed to meet the music's end, signifying the end to his performance and quest. Clive thrust his mandibles and maxillae towards the judges and crowd, with the mystique and an aura of a champion in waiting. The entire arena shook as raucous applause and cheers echoed; almost lifting the roof off. Bouquets of multi-coloured flowers littered the exasperated ice rink. Slowly, Clive took a tentative look at the score board.

It seemed to take an eternity…

… once again time froze…

… the judges conferred…

Clive and Albania's destiny in the hands of five devoted ice skating aficionados

… 6.0…6.0…6.0…6.0…6.0. The perfect score!

The arena erupted once more. The streets in Tirana exploded has thousands of people spilled onto the streets. Their champion had arrived! Clive the Albanian Ice skater was now…

…Clive, the Albanian, Olympic Gold Medallist, Ice Skating Sensation – fittingly a long name for an athlete with so many feet.

And what next for Clive the Albanian ice skating centipede? A generation to be inspired by his magnificent feet and feat? Children the world over racing to the nearest ice rink to follow in Clive's very many, many, many footsteps?

Well in the case of Albania's only Gold medallist. Only one thing: retire at the top and cash in on his fame with a lucrative Nike trainer sponsorship deal - of course!

An Even Shorter Short Story

The Real Woody The Woodpecker (The Very Short Story of…)

Each day Woody spends his time at school, making sure the children of Morton stay on task.

Every evening he goes home with a different child.

It was on one of these evenings that the real Woody Woodpecker started to reveal his true self.

Whilst walking from the park with Joel, a loud noise could be heard from up the top end of the village.

An oil tanker was speeding through and out of control.

At this very moment, a mother with her baby in a pram, was crossing that very same road.

The mother slipped. The pram was pushed into the middle of the road and as she fell, she screamed, " Aaargh, someone save my baby!"

Joel gasped in panic.

Woody immediately ripped open his jacket to reveal a red and blue outfit that had a 'SB' in the centre of his chest.

"Super Bird will save the day!" Cried Woody.

Without hesitation and a swoosh, Woody flew towards the pram like a bullet from a gun, his red cape trailing behind. The oil tanker was inching closer to the pram at 100 miles per hour. The mother screamed again, "Aaargh, someone save my baby!"

The world seemed to stop spinning as it awaited the fate of the unfortunate baby in the pram. Arriving in less than a split second, Woody expertly karate kicked the pram to the other side of the road.

The huge tanker missed the pram by millimetres; tyres screeched and the tanker suddenly stopped dead.

Woody emerged from the front of the truck, his wings smouldering. He had used his Super Bird strength and effortlessly held out his wings to bring the lorry to a halt.

He flew back over to Joel and said, " Wow, that was close. I wonder what we'll be doing at school tomorrow?"

Reviews – What the critics say

'Some of the best poems ever!' – **Andy Baines, Author.**

'His best book by far. Think it is his first too' – **J. Baines, Son.**

'I didn't know he could spell' – **O. Baines, Son.**

'He is rubbish at ironing' **L. Baines, Wife.**

'I like Roald Dahl better' – **R. Baines, Grandad.**

'Andy who?' – **Parents**

'I thrashed him at golf' – **A Goldfish**

'I love them all, the short ones and long ones. They are brilliant and fun. Are we talking about sticks?' – **Alfie, the family dog.**